TILLY'S PONY TAILS

Rusty
the
trustworthy pony

Pippa Funnell began riding when she was very young –
on a pony given to her by a friend of her mother's.

An Olympic champion, she became the first and (so far)
only person to win eventing's greatest prize, the Rolex
Grand Slam in 2003, riding Primmore's Pride.
She has had countless other successes in her career,
most recently winning the Bramham International Horse
Trials on Redesigned in June 2010. She's also delighted
to have been a member of the British team at the 2010
World Equestrian Games held in Kentucky.
Pippa is proud to be a trustee of World Horse Welfare.
Visit their website at www.worldhorsewelfare.org.

Tilly's Pony Tails mark her brilliant debut in
children's fiction. She lives in Surrey with her husband,
William Funnell, a top class show jumper.

Look at the back of the book
for a full list of all the books in the
Tilly's Pony Tails series

TILLY'S PONY TAILS

Rusty
the
trustworthy pony

PIPPA FUNNELL

Illustrated by Jennifer Miles

Orion
Children's Books

First published in Great Britain in 2011
by Orion Children's Books
a division of the Orion Publishing Group Ltd
Orion House
5 Upper St Martin's Lane
London WC2H 9EA
An Hachette UK Company

1 3 5 7 9 8 6 4 2

ISBN 978 1 4440 0261 4

Printed and bound in the UK by CPI Mackays, Chatham ME5 8TD

www.orionbooks.co.uk
www.tillysponytails.co.uk

To the RDA, for all their sterling work

One

It was late September, and though the sun was shining, early signs of autumn were beginning to show. As Tilly and Mia rode their horses along the bridle path, a scattering of golden-brown leaves fluttered in front of them.

'I love this time of year,' said Tilly.

'Me too,' said Mia.

She leaned forward and patted her chestnut horse.

'And it suits you perfectly.'

Mia's horse was called Autumn Glory. He was the colour of reddening leaves. Tilly's horse, Magic Sprit, was a grey, and his coat shone beautifully in the sunlight. They looked great together, walking side by side, while the girls chatted about next year's Pony Club camp.

After stopping for a rest at a small clearing, it was time to return to Silver Shoe Farm.

'Let's take the long route, around the back of the village,' suggested Tilly.

This was one of their favourite off-road tracks – a small lane that ran along the edge of North Cosford, with its big gardens and chestnut trees. Soon, they were out of the forest and on their way.

At the end of the track there was a little hump-backed bridge which crossed a stream. The horses could sometimes be nervous about the bridge, so Tilly and Mia paused to give them time to get used to it, then urged them forward. Autumn Glory crossed the bridge with no fuss,

but Magic remained reluctant.

'Come on, boy,' said Tilly. 'It's only a little stream. You've been over it a hundred times. We won't get home if you don't.'

She nudged with her leg, but he still wouldn't move. Magic could be stubborn with other people, but to refuse an instruction from Tilly was unusual.

'Is there something on the other side of the bridge, something that might be bothering him?' Tilly called.

Mia looked around.

'I can't see anything. It's just the same as always.'

Mia could sense Autumn growing impatient to move on. She patted his neck soothingly.

Tilly nudged Magic again, but he remained where he was. Then she heard a small whinny.

'What was that?' she said, puzzled. 'That wasn't you, was it, boy?'

Tilly kicked Magic with her leg one more time and finally he walked on. But as they approached the bridge, she heard the whinny again. It wasn't Magic, and Autumn was too far away for her to be able to hear him. So where was it coming from?

Intrigued, she moved Magic closer to the cobbled wall that backed onto the big gardens. She tried to peer over, but couldn't see any sign of a horse.

'It's Mrs Pollinger's garden,' said Tilly. 'That couldn't have been Rusty, could it?'

Mrs Pollinger was an old lady.

She lived at the house and kept a pony
called Rusty. She'd once been a rider, but
years ago she'd had an accident and had to
give it up. She'd never lost her love of horses
and ponies though, and she often stopped
by Silver Shoe Farm to say hello. She kept
Rusty in a small paddock at the bottom of
her garden. Sometimes the girls would stop
to lean over the wall and watch him.

They hadn't taken this route for a while
and today the wall was overgrown with
brambles. The garden – usually immaculate
– was messy and wild with weeds.

'That doesn't look good,' said Tilly.

Magic gave another snort. Mia and Autumn Glory came back over the bridge to see what was going on.

'What's up?'

'Take a look.'

Mia peered over the wall too.

'What am I supposed to be looking at? An overgrown hedge?'

Then the whinnying noise came again.

Autumn Glory and Magic pricked their ears.

'Where did that come from?' said Mia. 'It sounds as if it's right beside us.'

'I can't see Rusty in his field,' said Tilly, straining again to look over the wall.

They looked back along the path to see if any other riders were coming. It was quiet and empty.

'Maybe it was a ghost horse?' said Mia, pulling a silly face.

'Hang on a minute,' said Tilly.

She leaned up and forward in her saddle, hoping Magic would stay still long

12

enough for her to balance. She wanted
to get enough height to see over the wall
properly. Luckily, Magic obliged, and sure
enough, directly below, on the other side,
Tilly caught a glimpse of a dun-coloured
pony.

She sat back and stared at Mia.

'It *is* Rusty. He's right on the other side
of the wall.'

Rusty let out another whinny. Magic
made a wickering noise, as though he was
trying to let Rusty know they were close
by. Rusty whinnied again.

'Do you think he's okay?' said Mia.

'I don't know,' said Tilly.

'What's he doing in the garden?' said Mia. 'He must have got out of his paddock.'

'But did you see? Everything in the garden is a mess. I know it's been a while since we've been here, but something doesn't feel right.'

'What should we do?'

'Let's go round the front and see if Mrs Pollinger is in. She might not realise what's happened.'

Mia nodded. 'Sounds like a plan.'

'Come on then.'

Tilly nudged with her leg, and this time Magic walked straight over the bridge with no trouble. She leaned forward and gave him a pat.

'Thank you, boy. That's much more helpful.'

Two

Tilly and Mia made their way to the front
of the house. They tied their horses where
it was safe, away from the roadside, then
rang Mrs Pollinger's doorbell. There was no
response.

They rang again and waited. But still
nobody came.

'Maybe she's out?' said Tilly.

'I'll have a look through the window,'
said Mia.

She pressed her face against the glass.

'Oh!' she said, pulling back. 'It doesn't

look like Mrs Pollinger is there at all. The furniture is covered with dust sheets. It's a bit creepy. She must have gone away.'

'But what about Rusty?' said Tilly. She didn't like the thought of the little pony left in the garden to fend for himself. 'We should go and check he's all right.'

'Let's see if we can get round the back.'

The girls found a side-gate and walked into the overgrown garden. They had to tread carefully through the long grass. At the far side was a small paddock. The fence had part-collapsed, which explained why Rusty was now in the garden.

'There he is. We need to do things quietly and slowly to make sure we don't startle him,' said Tilly, remembering her work experience with World Horse Welfare. 'If this was a World Horse Welfare rescue mission, they'd assess the situation first.'

They stood back for a moment and watched.

'He's so little,' said Mia.

'I'd say 14.2hh at the most,' said Tilly.

'He doesn't look hungry – and he's in decent condition.'

'He's beautiful,' added Tilly. 'A classic dun Connemara.'

She admired his toffee-coloured coat. It was slightly dappled over his quarters. His mane and tail were black, as were his legs. There were no obvious signs of neglect – not like there had been with Goliath, the shire horse Tilly had helped rescue with the World Horse Welfare field officers – so if he *had* been left alone, it couldn't have been for long.

'Shall we go and say hello?' said Tilly. She was relieved now that she could see he was healthy.

'Let's do it.'

Tilly went first, approaching Rusty from the side so he wouldn't feel threatened. She made a low humming noise to let him know she was coming. Mia came behind her. As he became aware of them both, he pricked his ears and stared.

'Don't worry, Rusty,' said Tilly. 'Remember us? We've come to check you're okay. Looks like you've managed to get out of your field.'

Rusty whinnied again. It wasn't an aggressive sound. To Tilly, it sounded rather lonely. She reached out and hoped he would come towards her.

'It's okay,' she said reassuringly.

Rusty didn't move. Tilly stepped a bit closer. At last, Rusty sniffed her hand and nibbled her horsehair bracelets, just like Magic and some of the other horses sometimes liked to.

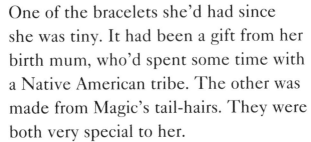

One of the bracelets she'd had since she was tiny. It had been a gift from her birth mum, who'd spent some time with a Native American tribe. The other was made from Magic's tail-hairs. They were both very special to her.

Rusty allowed Tilly to pat his neck. As Mia joined them, he nudged both their hands with his head. He obviously wanted some affection.

'He's so gentle and sweet,' said Mia. 'He must be sad all by himself.'

Tilly agreed. The thought of leaving him made her heart ache.

'At least it looks as though he's safe in this bit of the garden,' she said. 'And he's clearly not starving, so someone must be looking after him if it isn't Mrs Pollinger. Let's go back to Silver Shoe and tell Angela. She might want to come down and check things out for herself.'

Angela was Silver Shoe Farm's owner. She knew nearly everything there was to know about horses and the girls always respected her advice.

'Goodbye, Rusty. Someone will be back to see you soon.'

As they were leaving the garden gate they heard a lonely sounding whinny again.

'Let's hurry,' said Tilly.

Tilly and Mia found Angela in the yard. When they told her about Rusty, she immediately went to make some phone-calls. She knew the Pollinger house and thought it was very strange that the pony would be left on his own. The girls gave their horses a drink, then took them down to the long field to graze. They put their tack away and waited for Angela in the club room.

'I'm afraid it's not good news,' said Angela, as she joined them on the sofa. 'I've spoken to one of the neighbours. Mrs Pollinger passed away a fortnight ago.

She'd been in hospital for a while.'

'Oh,' said Mia. 'That's terrible.
No wonder Rusty seemed so unhappy.
He must be pining for her.'

'Yes, she'll be missed around here.
She was a lovely lady, but she was old and

frail – into her eighties. That's a good long life.'

'What will happen to Rusty?' said Tilly.

'Well, the neighbour had been helping to look after him. She'd been feeding him since Mrs Pollinger became ill, but now she's not sure what to do. She said Mrs Pollinger's son plans to sell the house, and when I spoke to him he said he definitely doesn't want responsibility for Rusty. He asked if I knew if anyone who would take a little pony, so . . .'

She paused.

Tilly had a feeling she knew what was coming next. 'I've agreed to have him here for the time being. Until Mr Pollinger can find another suitable home. I can just about squeeze him in.'

23

'Yesss!' said Tilly and Mia together.

'He's lovely,' said Mia.

'He's really good-natured,' said Tilly. 'You won't regret this.'

Three

Tilly and Mia worked together to get the spare stable ready for Rusty. Mr Magee, a small chestnut, who'd been kept there previously, was moved back to his old stable, which had needed a few repairs. Tilly and Mia gave the floor a thorough sweep, laid some fresh bedding, and put in a hay-net and a water bucket. They couldn't stop talking about what had happened that morning.

'I knew we'd done the right thing,' said Mia.

'It's so sad about Mrs Pollinger,' said
Tilly. 'It'll be strange not seeing her
around. But I'm glad Rusty is joining us.
The thought of him being on his own in
that great big garden is awful. At least he'll
make lots of new friends at Silver Shoe.'

Later, as Tilly crossed the yard, she noticed
one of the Silver Shoe regulars, Mr Magee's
owner, Lucy, struggling with her son,
Edward. Edward was refusing to walk to
Mr Magee's new stable. He was only a few
years younger than Tilly herself – too old to
be making such a fuss. He was screaming
and banging his fist against his head. She
didn't want to stare, but it was hard not to
notice.

'Edward,' said Lucy quietly, as she
tried to take a hold of his wrist to stop him
hurting himself. 'You have to calm down.
The horses will be frightened if you keep

making that kind of noise.'

'It's the wrong stable!' said Edward.
'You made Mr Magee go in the wrong
stable! I don't like it in there!'

'I know. I know,' said Lucy. 'But we've
had to make room for a new pony. Mr
Magee couldn't stay in the spare stable
forever. He's back in his old one now.
You like the old one, don't you?'

'I only like the spare stable!' said
Edward.

Tilly had seen Edward around the yard
before. She knew there was something
different about him – that he had some
kind of special needs – but she'd never
seen him get so worked up. She felt bad
for Lucy, who was trying her best to settle
Edward down, but looking tired and
frustrated herself.

Tilly had an idea. She went over to
them.

'Hi, Lucy. Hi, Edward. Um, Edward,
the tack room is in a bit of a mess, would
you mind coming to help me tidy it?'

Edward stopped screaming and looked at her.

'Why?' he said.

'It needs a good sort out,' she replied, with a shrug. 'It would be nice to have an extra pair of hands.'

Lucy nodded. 'That's a great idea. You're good at organising stuff, aren't you, Edward?'

She smiled at Tilly gratefully. They both knew she was perfectly capable of tidying the tack room herself, but at least she'd succeeded in distracting Edward.

Edward and Tilly walked together across the yard.

'Thanks,' said Tilly.

Edward nodded at her. His face was emotionless.

'Any time, Tiger Lily Redbrow,' he said.

Tilly was startled.

'I didn't know you knew my full name.'

'I know everyone's full name. I'm an expert in names. I know all the horses' names too. And I know where their stables are. Red Admiral is in number one, next to Lulabelle. Then there's Magic Spirit, who belongs to the stables, but is mostly ridden by you. His stable is next to Autumn Glory's. Autumn Glory is next to Parkview Pickle. Parkview Pickle is next to Mr Magee, I mean Mr Magee's old stable. Except, I don't like the old stable.'

'Maybe Mr Magee likes it?' said Tilly. 'Maybe he likes being next door to Pickle? It's nice to have company.'

'I don't like company.'

Sensing this discussion was going nowhere, Tilly ushered Edward into the tack room.

Later, Edward's mum stopped to talk to Tilly.

'Thanks so much for stepping in before. It really did the trick. Sometimes Ed can be a real handful.'

'It's okay,' said Tilly. 'It was interesting talking to him. He knows everything about Silver Shoe. I didn't realise he was so smart.'

'That's Edward. He remembers everything.'

'He doesn't like the fact that Mr Magee's stable has changed, does he?'

'No.' Lucy sighed. 'Edward is autistic, which means he can get stressed very easily. He finds it hard when his routine is changed – it makes him feel insecure.

He'd got used to seeing Mr Magee in a certain place and the change has unsettled him. He'll be fine with it eventually. It'll just take a while to adjust.'

Tilly nodded. This made sense. There was a boy in her class called Roger who was autistic. He had extra support and found it difficult to concentrate. The only thing that seemed to hold his attention was the cartoon channel, which he was obsessed with. He carried a cartoon lunch box everywhere and always wanted to talk about his favourite characters.

Tilly glanced over at Edward, who now seemed absorbed in counting the number of fence posts he could see. She guessed that remembering things was his version of Roger's cartoons.

'Does Edward like coming to Silver Shoe?' she asked.

'He loves it. I haven't managed to get him riding yet – he's too frightened – but he enjoys being around the horses and helping me look after Mr Magee.

It's a shame he won't ride though, because I think he'd get a lot out of it. Riding and building a relationship with a horse, or any animal, can be really beneficial for autistic children. That's what our specialist says anyway.'

Tilly smiled. She thought she vaguely remembered reading something similar in one of her pony magazines. She'd have to look it up.

Four

Rusty arrived later that afternoon. Tilly and Mia helped Angela lead him out of the horsebox. He seemed calm, despite the journey and the confusion of being somewhere new. He walked down the ramp into the yard and gave a little nicker.

'I think he likes it here,' said Mia.

'He seems content,' said Tilly. It was nice to hear him make a happy sound, rather than that lonely whinny.

'I think he's the sort of horse that

would be happy anywhere,' said Angela. 'You were right. He's lovely. He has a very gentle spirit. And he definitely likes being around people.'

'He seemed desperate for some company when we saw him,' said Mia.

'Poor Rusty,' said Tilly, stroking his neck. He looked at her with his big, brown eyes. 'You'll have plenty of people to hang out with at Silver Shoe,' she said. 'Shall we show you to your stable?'

'Good idea,' said Angela. 'I'd better complete his paperwork and give the vet a call. I'd like to find out a little more about his background too. Let me know how he settles.'

Tilly and Mia led Rusty to his stable. As they crossed the yard, Tilly noticed Edward watching them from a nearby bench. She gave him a wave but he didn't respond, although he kept his eyes on them the entire time.

It was a windy day and as they approached Rusty's stable, a strong breeze blew an empty bag of shavings across their path. Tilly and Mia stopped to make sure Rusty was okay, but he didn't even flinch. They couldn't believe it.

'This is your new home, for now anyway,' said Mia, as they reached the stable door. 'I'm sorry that was a bit of a scary welcome, but you didn't seem worried by it at all!'

'You'll spend lots of time here as well as in the field,' added Tilly. 'The horses at Silver Shoe get to exercise and graze as much as possible. It's good for your health. But with winter not far away – you'll appreciate a cosy stable at night.'

She gave Rusty a reassuring pat, undid the bolt and led him inside.

'You have fresh water, bedding, and hay if you're hungry,' Mia explained.

Rusty sniffed the ground, then the walls. He turned, then went straight to his hay-net and began to munch. He looked comfortable already.

Suddenly, there was another gust of wind and a loud noise echoed around the stable block. Mia and Tilly jumped. The metal dustbin which sat in the corner of the yard had crashed over and swept across

the ground. Again, Rusty didn't react at all.
A different horse might have been startled
by the noise, but Rusty just stood there, as
though nothing had happened.

'He's not fazed by much, is he?' said
Mia. 'I'll go and find him some carrots.
See if he likes those.'

She disappeared through the door into
the daylight, leaving Tilly and Rusty alone.

'Well,' said Tilly. 'I didn't even know
you properly when I woke up this morning

and now here you are, settling into a stable at Silver Shoe Farm. I'm so pleased we heard you on the path, otherwise you might still be in that garden on your own.'

Rusty stopped eating the hay and turned towards her. He held himself very gracefully. He had a small, delicate face and his eyes seemed to smile. Tilly smiled back. There was something about him that reminded her of Neptune, the beach horse she'd met while on holiday in Cornwall with her brother, Brook.

Tilly recognised in Rusty the same special quality that Neptune had had – a calm strength that was reassuring to anyone in the saddle. She stroked his velvety nose.

'I can't wait to get to know you better,' she whispered. 'I bet you're capable of amazing things.'

She ran her hand across his coat. It was in good condition, although she knew with a thorough groom, she could have it gleaming.

'What about a brush down?' she suggested. 'The vet will be here soon, then I'll do it for you, I promise. I'll go and get a grooming kit now.'

Tilly went straight to the tack room to collect some brushes. She wouldn't use

Magic's or any other horse's grooming gear. It was one of Angela's rules that any new horse or pony had to be brushed with separate brushes for their first week at Silver Shoe. This was a precaution in case they had ringworm or another skin infection that might spread to the other horses. Luckily Angela always kept spares of everything and made sure they were regularly cleaned with disinfectant. She found a selection of brushes for Rusty's mane and tail. She also found a hoof pick and a cloth.

When she returned to Rusty's stable, she saw that the top half of the door had been closed, along with the bottom half. That wasn't how she'd left it. She heard a shuffling sound and the quiet murmur of a voice. Was Mia in there with him? Tilly thought it odd that Mia would have shut the stable door completely. Then she saw her emerging from the shed with a handful of carrots.

Who was in the stable then?

Puzzled, she opened the door and looked inside. Edward was standing beside Rusty. His head was resting on the little pony's back and he was running his hands along the length of his body in gentle, rhythmic movements. He looked peaceful, but when he saw Tilly, he jumped, and pushed past her out of the stable.

'Who was that?' said Mia, coming up behind.

'It was Edward,' said Tilly.

'Lucy's son? What was he doing?'

'I'm not sure. Saying hello to Rusty, I guess.'

Tilly shrugged. She glanced at Rusty, who seemed just as content as when she'd left him, then back towards Edward, who was running away through the yard. She remembered her conversation with Lucy that morning, and suddenly she had an idea.

Five

Next day at school Tilly had one of her
favourite lessons, Geography. They were
learning about streams and rivers. As
the teacher talked, she imagined herself
galloping into the water on Magic Spirit,
with Mia and Autumn Glory alongside.
She closed her eyes for a moment and
thought she could almost feel the spray
splashing up into her face.

'Wake up, Tilly. Earth to Planet Pony!'
hissed her friend Becky, next to her.

She gave Tilly a nudge.

'I wasn't asleep. I was – oh, never mind.'

Towards the end of the lesson she noticed Roger, the autistic boy in her class. She'd never really thought much about autism before, but since she'd been getting to know Edward, and was starting to think about how she could help him, she found herself watching to see how Roger behaved. He was sitting at the back of the classroom with his helper. She could see he was getting restless, fidgeting in his seat and making little noises. Clearly, he'd had enough of streams and rivers. And actually, so had Tilly. Eventually Roger tried to stand up and the teacher, Mrs Cardew, went over to talk to him. She asked him to sit down, but he began to bang his lunch box on the desk, and even his helper couldn't do anything to calm him down. In the end, Mrs Cardew allowed Roger and his helper to leave the room early.

After the lesson, Tilly hung back. She

wanted to ask Mrs Cardew some questions.

'Hi, Tilly, how can I help?'

'I was wondering about Roger, about autism, Miss.'

'Oh, really?'

'What is it? I mean, what does it actually mean if someone has it?'

'It's a special disorder that affects the way people communicate. Some people, like Roger, have it quite mildly and just need a bit of help getting on with day-to-day life. Others have greater difficulties and aren't able to talk or look after themselves.'

Tilly thought about Edward. He was pretty capable. In fact, he seemed pretty clever with all the counting and memorising he did.

'Autistic people can be really smart, can't they?'

'Of course. I once knew a child who collected football cards. He had hundreds. He would spend hours lining them up in an order and he could remember each one.'

45

That sounded a bit like Edward.

'Why do autistic people get stressed out so easily?'

'It could be a number of things. Change or disruption to routine can be unsettling. Or it could be a situation they don't like or find frightening. Some autistic people have heightened senses, so loud noises or certain smells, tastes and textures can make them feel very uncomfortable.'

Tilly thought of Silver Shoe. There were always strong smells there. She loved the scent of saddle oil, hay, the leather of Magic's tack, even the horse manure. But she wondered what Edward thought of it all. His mum, Lucy, had told her he enjoyed coming to the farm, so maybe the smells and sounds didn't bother him. And even if he was frightened of riding, he obviously loved being around horses, from the way he'd been stroking Rusty. Tilly looked up at Mrs Cardew.

'I heard that spending time with animals can help people with autism.

Do you think that's true?'

'It's an interesting question, Tilly. I'm impressed that you've given this so much thought.'

'There's a boy at my riding stables,' she explained. 'He's autistic, like Roger.'

'Well, to answer you, yes, I think there has been some evidence to suggest being around animals might be helpful. They seem to have a kind of calming influence.'

Tilly thought about how good it felt to arrive at Silver Shoe after school each day. It was instant relaxation, a place where she could let any worries melt away and just enjoy being with Magic.

'Definitely,' she said.

Mrs Cardew pushed her glasses up her nose.

'Autistic people often have difficulties expressing feelings and getting on with other people, so they might find it easier with animals.'

'Is that why Roger never seems to want to make friends?'

'Exactly. It can be a very lonely world.'

Tilly smiled.

'Thanks for your help, Miss.'

'No problem. Let me know how you and your friend get on, won't you?'

That evening, Tilly was in the sand school at Silver Shoe, having a jump with Magic. Duncan, Angela's head boy, was watching her, giving helpful hints.

'Getting better each time, Tilly! Keep those hands still and don't rush. Take your time to get straight, don't cut the corners.'

Tilly circled and made a turn, which enabled her to have a straighter approach to the triple bar. She loved the feeling. It was a big jump, a real challenge, and it was great getting it right.

'That was pretty stylish!' called Angela, as she approached the sand school. 'I came over to tell you some good news.'

Tilly and Magic trotted up and stopped by the post-and-rail fencing.

'What is it?'

'I've just had a phone call from Mrs Pollinger's son. Apparently, his mother was a big supporter of Riding for the Disabled, and she's left a significant amount of money to them. And she's also left them Rusty. They're not sure where he'll be placed yet, but at least he'll have a good future ahead of him.'

'That's great,' said Duncan.

Tilly loved the idea of Rusty becoming an RDA pony. It would suit his calm nature perfectly. But she hoped it wouldn't happen too quickly. First, she wanted Edward and Rusty to spend some time together.

Six

On Saturday, Tilly spent the whole day at Silver Shoe. Her dad dropped her off in the morning. As she climbed out of the car he caught her eye.

'You're looking very thoughtful today, Tiger Lil'. What's up?'

Tilly flashed a smile.

'I've got a plan,' she said. 'I've been doing lots of research, and today I'm going to put my plan into action!'

'Sounds interesting. Does it involve horses?'

'Of course.'

'Ask a silly question. Good luck. See you later.'

After feeding, grooming and mucking out, and a long, leisurely ride with Magic, Tilly went to find Edward. He was sitting on an up-turned bucket in the yard, talking to himself, and counting on his fingers. He looked as though he was concentrating hard.

'Hi,' said Tilly.

Edward said hello, but he didn't look up and carried on with his counting.

'What are you doing?' Tilly continued. 'Can I join you?'

She crouched beside him and hoped it wouldn't bother him. Lucy had told her that he didn't like people to come too close.

'Are you working out where all the horses are stabled today?'

'All the horses,' he repeated, finally acknowledging her properly. 'Lulabelle next to Red Admiral. Magic next to

Autumn Glory. Rusty in the spare stable.'

He paused for a minute.

'I like Rusty.'

'I know,' said Tilly. 'I saw you with him the other day, remember? You ran away so quickly, I didn't get a chance to ask you about it.'

'I wasn't doing anything wrong,' said Edward. 'Just stroking. I like Rusty.'

Tilly smiled.

'I'm glad,' she said. 'He's a great pony. I'm sure he liked the attention you were giving him. Would you like to go and see him now? We could go together.'

'Yes,' said Edward, in a matter-of-fact voice. 'Let's go and see Rusty.'

'He might still be in his stable,' said Tilly, standing up. 'I'll check.'

'Not in his stable,' said Edward. 'Angela took him down to the long field at ten thirty-one, while you were getting a hot chocolate drink in the club room.'

'R-r-right,' said Tilly, amazed that Edward picked up on so much detail. 'We'll head for the long field then.'

They found Rusty, just as Edward had said, grazing in the long field with a few other horses and ponies. Parkview Pickle was there, and Buttons – the little pony who'd joined the farm a few months ago.

When he'd first arrived he'd been very
badly behaved. He'd refused to let his
owner, Tim, ride him, and had given
Angela and Duncan no end of trouble.
With a bit of help from Tilly and Jack
Fisher, Angela's dad, they'd discovered
Buttons much preferred being a driving
pony and pulling a trap to carrying a rider.
Now he was a reformed character.

Tilly waved as she watched Tim catch
Buttons and lead him to the gate.

'Going for a drive?' she called to him.

'Yes. We've got a competition coming up in a couple of weeks. Want to come along?'

'Thanks. I'm a bit busy at the moment.' She glanced at Edward, who was leaning over the fence, trying to call Rusty. 'Maybe later?'

'Hello, Rusty,' said Edward quietly. Tilly saw that Rusty had noticed Edward and was looking in his direction, but the pony didn't move towards him.

'Try holding out your hand,' Tilly suggested. 'And clicking your fingers. Make it really clear that you want Rusty to come to you. And raise your voice a bit. Make it sound encouraging.'

She demonstrated and Edward copied. He shouted Rusty's name and held his arm out, but it didn't look very convincing. Tilly remembered what her teacher, Mrs Cardew, had said about people with autism finding it hard to express feeling and emotion.

But to her surprise, Rusty responded. He came straight towards Edward and began to nuzzle his arm. The tension in Edward's face disappeared. He didn't quite smile, but his frown softened. His shoulders dropped and his arms relaxed.

Rusty stood side on and sniffed Edward's neck. He seemed to enjoy Edward's company as much as Edward enjoyed his. Tilly couldn't be certain, but she thought she heard Edward give a little

giggle. He didn't appear anxious, even though Rusty's face and nose were very close to his. Suddenly, Edward leaned over the fence and did the same thing Tilly had seen him do in the stable when Rusty had first arrived. He spread his arms wide across Rusty's back, leaned his head against his soft coat and shut his eyes.

Tilly didn't say anything. She didn't need to. And she realised she didn't have to try to encourage Edward and Rusty to bond. They already had.

Seven

'You obviously love horses but your mum told me you've never ridden before,' said Tilly, when Edward finally pulled away from Rusty's back. 'Is that true?'

'Not riding.' Edward shook his head. 'No horse is safe.'

'What about Rusty? Do you think he feels safe?'

Edward thought for a moment. He looked at Rusty then back at Tilly.

'Maybe,' he said. 'I trust Rusty.'

Tilly smiled.

'I trust him too. Why don't we try and get you up in the saddle? We'll ask your mum. And if she says yes, I'll help you. I think she'd be really pleased if she saw you riding.'

'Mum pleased. That would be good.'

'Come on then.'

Together, Tilly and Edward put a head collar and lead rope on Rusty and led him back to the yard, looking out for Edward's mum on the way. Tilly kept her fingers crossed. She really hoped Lucy would agree to let Edward ride Rusty. If the research she'd done was correct, it would help

build his confidence and trust, not just in animals, but in people too.

As Tilly tied Rusty in the yard, Lucy walked by, with her horse, Mr Magee.

'Oh, hi, Tilly. There you are, Ed. I was wondering where you'd got to.'

'Sorry, Lucy. It's my fault,' said Tilly. 'We went down to the long field to see Rusty. I didn't realise he was supposed to be waiting for you.'

'That's okay, Tilly. I know he's safe wherever he is in Silver Shoe, because everyone knows him and looks out for him. But I was worried he'd left the farm. Anyway, no harm done. You went to see Rusty, did you, Ed?'

'Yes, Rusty. I like Rusty. I trust Rusty. Tilly says I can ride Rusty.'

'Er.' Tilly floundered. 'I said we'll ask your mum.'

'Yes,' said Edward emphatically. 'Ask.'

'You *actually* want to ride?' said Lucy. She looked surprised, but a bit worried too. 'Well. That's great.'

'Can we get him in some riding gear then? Give it a try?' said Tilly. 'I said I'd help. The way they are together, they really get on. I think they'd be fine. We could both supervise. Or I could ask Angela?'

'Why not?' said Lucy. 'I've wanted Ed to try riding for ages, but he's always been too afraid before, and I've never been able to convince him to give it a go. He seems somehow . . . *calmer* today. Maybe it's worth a go.'

Lucy took Mr Magee back to his stable while Tilly and Edward went to the tack room. Edward knew the name and brand of every single piece of equipment, including all the different bridles and bits. He even knew, without reading the name labels, which horses they belonged to.

'Try this,' said Tilly, handing him a spare riding hat. It fitted perfectly. Edward was already wearing jodhpur boots so he was ready.

'Now for Rusty's tack,' said Tilly. 'This is his saddle. Angela brought it over from Mrs Pollinger's house. Wow!'

She admired the quality of the leather.

'It's a really expensive one. Lucky Rusty. I guess Mrs Pollinger had quite a bit of money – some of which is going to the RDA now.'

'What's RDA?' said Edward.

'It's the Riding for the Disabled Association. Rusty will make a good RDA pony, because he's so sweet and steady, don't you think?'

'Am I disabled?'

'Um, sort of.' Tilly wasn't sure how to answer this.

'I go to a special school for disabled children. I like Rusty. I don't want Rusty to go to RDA. I'd like Rusty to come to my school.'

Tilly frowned. She realised she didn't want to be the one to tell Edward that Rusty would soon be leaving Silver Shoe to become an RDA pony.

Edward watched as Tilly and Lucy tacked Rusty up. He told them where to put everything and how much to tighten the straps, then how to adjust them.

For someone who'd never ridden before,
he certainly knew his stuff.

They led Rusty to the sand school, which
was quiet after the morning's lessons. Lucy
thought it would be good to avoid other
riders or potential noises and distractions
– not because they'd bother Rusty, but
because they might upset Edward.

Angela was waiting for them. 'Hi, guys. So you're trying your first ride today, Edward? Well just try to relax, have fun and enjoy it. I'm on hand to keep an eye, but otherwise I'll leave you in Tilly's capable hands.'

Tilly felt her cheeks go slightly pink. She was proud that Angela put so much trust in her.

'Okay,' she explained, as they stood in the centre of the sand school. 'The first thing you need to do is prepare to mount. Take your time. We can practise first. Then, if you stand to the side, Rusty will stay perfectly still and you can get your left foot in the stirrup.'

'I know,' said Edward impatiently.

While Lucy kept hold of the lead rein, Edward went round to Rusty's side. Without hesitation, and without practising, he put his left foot in the stirrup, swung his right leg over Rusty's back and settled into the saddle. It was as though it was second nature to him.

'Well done, Ed!'

Tilly, Lucy and Angela looked at each other. They were amazed.

'I guess he's watched me do it so many times,' said Lucy. 'Sometimes I forget how much he takes in. I wouldn't be surprised if he trots off now and completes three perfect circuits.'

As she spoke, Lucy felt a slight pull on the reins. Edward was kicking with his foot.

'I'm ready to go, Mum. You can let go now.'

'No, Ed. I'll lead you,' said Lucy. 'And Tilly will walk beside you. We need to make sure you're okay.'

'I'm already okay,' said Edward. 'I'll be fine with Rusty.'

Before Edward could protest any further, the group set off. Rusty made it easy and was very responsive to Lucy, as the leader. He even seemed to understand that he had to listen to Lucy above Edward, who was keen to give Rusty his own instructions and ride independently.

'Wow,' said Angela. 'I'm impressed.'

Edward and Rusty completed a flawless circuit of the sand school. Tilly couldn't believe how natural it looked. Edward had an excellent sense of balance. He was very upright in the saddle and did things correctly. He kept his arms and hands relaxed and his legs straight.

Tilly looked at Lucy. She was smiling from ear-to-ear, and Tilly thought she saw a tear in her eye. She was clearly delighted. Watching Edward, it was hard to believe he'd never been on a horse before. He seemed so comfortable. Of course, much of that was thanks to Rusty, who made it look it effortless.

Eight

On Sunday, Tilly met her friends, Mia and Cally, and her brother, Brook. Together they went hacking with their horses. They'd planned a trip to the Lost Pond, which Duncan had recommended. Tilly had looked forward to it all week. It was down forest tracks, a long way from roads and traffic.

The air was cold but the sky was clear blue, as their horses, Magic Spirit, Autumn Glory, Mr Fudge, and Brook's splendid black thoroughbred, Solo, walked along the track. The leaves on the trees had turned gold and red. They were beginning to flutter to the ground, but the horses didn't seem to mind. They enjoyed riding through the countryside, whatever the season.

Tilly and Brook went ahead side-by-side.

'How's your training going?' Tilly asked. She knew Brook had been working hard with Solo and was hoping to enter some big competitions next year.

'Good, thanks, although I'm really tired at the moment. I've got so much school work to get through, as well as riding. There are mock exams and coursework deadlines coming up. Sometimes I wonder when I'm going to fit it all in.'

'Don't worry,' said Tilly. 'I know you. You'll find a way. Is there anything I can do to help?'

'Thanks. But I'll get through it – somehow.'

Eventually the path split into three. The four friends stopped and worked out which way to go.

'According to Duncan's instructions,' said Mia, 'we need to take the left fork and then the pond should be a bit further along.'

They walked single file down the next path, which was narrower.

'Watch you don't get scratched!' warned Cally, as holly bushes brushed against their legs. 'Are we *sure* this is the right way?'

But as she said this, their destination appeared in front of them – a beautiful, quiet pond in the middle of a clearing. There was no one else around, just the sound of leaves crunching under the horses' hooves and the occasional *tap-tap-tap* of a woodpecker.

'It's lovely,' said Tilly. 'Worth the journey. Shall we have lunch here? I'm so hungry!'

'Good idea.'

The friends dismounted. With lead ropes, they tied their horses to nearby trees, then sat on a large rock overlooking the pond and got out their sandwiches.

'I wish we had some hot chocolate,' said Mia. 'I'm wearing my warmest riding gloves and my fingers have still gone numb. I'm going to have to start wearing two pairs soon.'

'That reminds me,' said Tilly. 'I put a flask in Brook's backpack just before we left.'

'Good thinking,' said Mia. 'You're always so organised.'

Tilly pulled out the flask along with her latest copy of *Pony* magazine.

'Even better!' said Mia, taking the magazine. 'I want some new riding gear for Christmas. They always have good ideas in here.'

She began to flick through it.

Brook turned to Cally.

'What are you up to this Christmas, Cal? Are you going to your parents'?'

'Yes, I'm off to Dubai. I can't wait. It's going to be really hot. And they promised they'd take me to the races.'

'All those gorgeous Arabian horses!' said Tilly.

'I wish I was going somewhere hot,' said Brook. 'Away from exam stress!'

'Maybe you can,' said Mia. 'Check this out.'

She held up the magazine.

'It's a competition, to win a trip on an African horseback safari in Botswana.'

'Wow!' said Tilly. 'That would be incredible.'

'Sounds great,' said Brook.

'We should enter,' said Cally. 'All you have to do is send in a photo of you and your favourite horse. If yours is the one they pick, you win. I bet you've got loads of pictures of you and Magic at home. I know I've got plenty of Mr Fudge.'

'Maybe,' said Tilly, making a mental note to take a closer look at the competition details later. 'Let's have some of that hot chocolate.'

They sat by the pond for another hour. It was fun just relaxing and hanging out together, despite the cold weather. The horses grazed and made soft nickering

sounds to one another, happy in their own company.

'I guess we'd better get going,' said Brook. 'It's starting to get dark earlier now and we don't want to be on the road at dusk.'

They gathered up their things, careful to remove all their rubbish. As they approached the horses, Brook stopped to admire their shiny coats and how well they all looked.

'They're so impressive,' he said.

Tilly agreed. She couldn't help feeling proud of Magic. It was good to hear him described as impressive, especially because, when he'd first arrived at Silver Shoe, after being rescued from a roadside in North Cosford, nobody had known what would happen to him. Now, he was a handsome grey with top class potential.

Nine

Tilly and Mia said goodbye to Cally and Brook at the gates of Cavendish Hall, the boarding school they both attended.

'See you soon,' said Brook.

'Don't forget to enter that competition,' said Cally. 'I'm going to do it now!'

'Bye.'

Tilly, Mia, Magic and Autumn walked together the rest of the journey, back to Silver Shoe. The sun was big and red and it sat low in the grey sky. A sweet smell of wood-fire smoke drifted through the air.

'More hot chocolate,' said Mia. 'I need warming up. Let's get to the club room fast.'

'We could go in the back entrance,' Tilly suggested, as they got near. 'It would be quicker from here.'

'Good idea.'

They headed for the disused track, which lead to the back of the yard. The horses were a little confused when the girls asked them to turn, because the track was rarely used and they'd been expecting to take the familiar route home. But with a bit of cajoling, they walked forward.

Soon they could see Silver Shoe's familiar cluster of white buildings – the farm house and the stable blocks. Tilly felt Magic's pace quicken when he recognised where they were going.

'That's it, boy. We're nearly back. When we reach the yard we'll get you a nice drink and something to eat. We might need to get rugs for you guys tonight.

It's going to be chilly.'

'Definitely,' said Mia, who'd been moaning about her cold hands and face since they'd left the forest.

As they got closer to the farm, the figure of a horse and rider appeared on the track ahead of them. They were too far away to see clearly, but there was definitely someone.

'Who's that?' said Mia. 'Why are they just standing at the edge of the track?'

'I can't tell,' said Tilly. 'It doesn't look like a very big horse. Probably a pony. Maybe it's Cynthia and Pickle come to greet us?'

'Maybe,' said Mia. 'But how would they know we came this way? And why would they be coming out now? It's getting dark.'

'Good point,' said Tilly.

As they approached, the pony and rider didn't move. It looked as though they had been waiting there for some time. Magic gave a little snort, as if he too was suspicious.

'Oh no!' whispered Tilly, as they finally drew close enough to identify the mystery figures. 'It's Edward and Rusty! I don't know what's going on, but I don't think they should be there. It looks as though they're on their own.'

'Disaster!' cried Mia. 'You said Edward had never ridden before you helped him yesterday. We've got to stop him!'

Tilly put her hand on Mia's arm.

'We can't rush in,' said Tilly. 'We have to stay calm and quiet.'

'But . . .'

'From what Edward's mum told me, he can get quite stressed out by unexpected things, sudden noises, that sort of stuff. We don't want to upset him while he's sitting in the saddle.'

'You're right,' said Mia. 'So what do we do?'

Tilly thought for a moment. She knew Rusty was unlikely to rear or buck, so she wasn't worried about that. But she didn't know how much Edward understood about riding commands.

'I think I should go and talk to him,' she said. 'On my feet rather than with Magic. I'll walk ahead. Can you bring the horses behind?'

'Okay,' said Mia.

They both dismounted. Tilly reassured Magic, then handed his reins to Mia.

Edward and Rusty didn't move as Tilly came towards them. When Edward saw her he didn't smile or wave.

'Hi, Edward,' she said calmly. 'I've just been riding with Magic and Mia and Autumn. What are you doing out here?'

'He's stopped,' said Edward, indignant.

'What do you mean?'

'Rusty. He won't go anywhere. I keep trying to make him go but he won't. Ponies are supposed to go.'

Tilly looked into Rusty's eyes and suddenly realised what must have

happened. Edward had mounted Rusty,
probably without anyone knowing, and
tried to take him down the track. Rusty,
being the sensible little pony he was, had
decided not to go any further.

'It's okay,' said Tilly, patting Rusty's
shoulder. 'Sometimes a pony knows it's not
a good idea to go too far, so they stand still.
Look, why don't you let me take his reins

so I can lead him back to the farm? Then he'll go again, you'll see.'

'But I want to go down the track,' said Edward. 'Rusty and I are going for an adventure.'

'Oh,' said Tilly. 'Well maybe we can go tomorrow, or another day. It's getting dark now, so it won't be much fun. Let's go and find your mum. Then we can talk to her about when we might be able to go for a hack.'

Edward nodded slowly and passed Tilly the reins.

She turned to Mia and gave a thumbs-up, then lead Rusty round in a circle and back through the entrance to the farm.

When they got to the yard, Tilly helped Edward dismount.

'You're so clever, Tilly Redbrow,' he said. 'You made Rusty go.'

'I think Rusty's the clever one,' said Tilly, with a smile.

Just then, Lucy and Angela came rushing out of the club room.

'There you are!' said Lucy, pulling
Edward into a hug. 'We've been so
worried! We were about to send out a
search party!'

'You told your mum you were going
to stay in the tack room and count the
bridles,' said Angela.

'Thank you so much for bringing him
back, Tilly. Where did you find him?' said
Lucy.

'He was out on the dirt track at the
back, on Rusty. Luckily, it looks as if Rusty
refused to go any further. I don't know how
long they'd been there.'

'Too long,' said Lucy. 'Edward you
mustn't ride without permission and you
mustn't disappear without telling anyone
where you are.'

Edward didn't say anything. He was
busy rubbing Rusty's neck.

Ten

Now that it was clear that Edward was safe, Angela said she had some important news about Rusty. Tilly thought she looked very pleased with herself.

'I've been talking to the people at Riding for the Disabled. They're coming to collect him tomorrow afternoon. They have a fantastic new home lined up, although I'm afraid it means Rusty's stay here is going to be cut short.'

Edward was out of ear-shot in the tack room. Tilly sighed, half-happy for Rusty, half-sad for what he was leaving behind. She knew Edward would be upset. Saying goodbye to such a special pony was going to be difficult for him. After all, she found it hard to leave Magic for a few days. She couldn't begin to imagine how it would feel if he left Silver Shoe completely.

'I know Rusty will do brilliantly as an RDA pony,' she said. 'What happened today proves it. He's so sensible and trustworthy. It's just a shame he has to go so soon. I feel as if we're only just getting to know him.'

'I'll have to break the news to Edward gently,' said Lucy. 'He'll be so disappointed.'

Angela gave them a big smile.

'But you haven't heard the best bit,' she said. 'Rusty isn't going far at all. A friend of mine works at Grange Farm, the local RDA centre, which is just on the other side of North Cosford. When I told her about Rusty she got in touch with the RDA head office and arranged for him to be placed there. I told her about Edward too, and she said they'd happily set up some riding lessons for him with Rusty. They'll teach him everything – horse care, riding skills, tack, and listening to instructions. He'll be able to get qualifications and certificates too.'

'That sounds brilliant,' said Lucy. 'Thank you so much, Angela.'

'Edward will be their star student,' said Tilly. 'He already knows plenty.'

She stroked Rusty's neck.

'That'll be good, won't it, boy? Come on, let's get this tack off you.'

She led him to the other end of the yard and tied him to a post. She was impressed that Edward – even though he shouldn't have done it without asking permission – had fitted Rusty's tack perfectly. Everything was tight and properly buckled.

'I've got high hopes for you,' she whispered, as she removed Rusty's bridle. 'You were such a clever little pony today, not taking Edward too far down the lane.'

She stroked his nose and looked into his eyes. They were bright and happy. She remembered how lonely he'd sounded when she and Mia had first discovered him, all alone in Mrs Pollinger's garden.

'I know you must miss Mrs Pollinger,' she said. 'But you've got a lovely new life ahead of you. You'll be busy at Grange Farm. I think you'll love it.'

Rusty rubbed his head on her shoulder and gave a little nicker. Tilly fetched him some fresh water and gave him a quick brush down.

'If you don't mind,' she said, working the brush along his sides and running her fingers through his tail. 'I might take some of these. I have a special bracelet to make.'

The following day after school, Angela's friends from Grange Farm arrived with a large horsebox. Tilly was down at the long field with Magic when Mia came to get her.

'They're here,' she called. 'Let's go and say goodbye.'

Tilly gave Magic a hug.

'I'll see you later, boy,' she said, feeling suddenly glad that it wasn't Magic she had to say goodbye to. She followed Mia back to the yard.

Edward and Lucy had already joined Angela and were talking to the Grange Farm people.

'Hi, guys,' said Angela. She introduced

them all. 'This is my friend, Mischa, and this is Ben.'

'Hi,' said Mischa. 'We're so grateful Rusty is coming to us. We're always looking for special ponies and horses to work with.'

'Tilly and Mia were the ones who discovered Rusty and suggested I check it out,' Angela explained. 'So it's thanks to them, really. Shall we go and find Rusty?'

She led them over to his stable.

Tilly and Mia stayed back with Lucy and Edward.

'Do you think Edward will be okay?' Tilly asked Lucy quietly. She'd been worried he would be upset, but he didn't seem too bothered. He was sitting on a nearby bench reading a manual about horse riding.

'We've had a good chat about it and he understands,' said Lucy. 'He was much calmer than I thought he'd be – but he's calmer generally, I think. Rusty's influence I'm sure. And yours. I can't wait to see how regular riding lessons will help him.'

Tilly went over to Edward.

'Hey,' she said. 'That looks like a good book.'

'I'm preparing for my lessons,' said Edward. 'I'll be riding Rusty every week from now on. I'm going to Grange Farm with Mischa and Ben. I'm going to be the best.'

'I bet you are,' said Tilly, smiling.

'Here,' she said, fishing into her pocket. 'I made you this.'

She gave him the bracelet.

'I made it from Rusty's tail-hairs,' she explained. 'I wear two, you see. This one was given to me by my birth mum. And this one is from Magic's tail-hairs. I made one for Mia too, from Autumn's tail, because he's her special horse. Rusty is your special pony – that's why I made one for you.'

'Did you hurt him?' he said.

'No. They were the loose hairs, from when I combed his tail. He didn't mind at all.'

'I like Rusty,' said Edward.

'And he likes you.'

When he said goodbye to Rusty, Edward leaned into his side and brushed his hands across his body, just as Tilly had seen him do before. He stayed there for a few seconds, then turned to Tilly.

'Now you,' he said.

She realised he meant she should copy him, so she leaned forward, pressed her head to Rusty's side and stretched out her arms. She felt the warmth of Rusty's body and the softness of his coat. She could see why Edward liked to be close to Rusty in this way. There was something very calming about it.

Rusty went into the horsebox happily, taking everything in his stride just as he'd done when he'd first arrived at the farm. As the horsebox drove away, they all stood waving.

'Well,' said Angela. 'That must be one of the shortest stays at Silver Shoe Farm that we've ever had.'

'Yes,' said Tilly. 'It has been quick.'

She looked over at Edward, who was carefully examining his horsehair bracelet.

'But it's one that's made a real difference.'

Then, for the first time since she'd known him, Edward looked up and smiled directly at her. And Tilly smiled back.

Pippa's Top Tips

Always take precautions when new horses or ponies come into a yard. Check for any signs of infection, disease, or flu-like symptoms and try to isolate them if this is the case.

To prevent infection, regularly clean brushes, preferably with disinfectant.

Make sure numnahs and boots/bandages are frequently washed. A numnah with dry sweat or other dirt will cause irritation to your pony's back, and dirty boots could irritate his legs.

If you have to ride in poor light or at dusk, make sure you are wearing something that will be highly visible to other road users.

Always try to go out hacking with a friend or in company. If you are going alone, get permission from your parents or guardian first and let them know exactly where you're planning to go. But even then I would not advise it.

Regularly check your pony's surroundings. For example, ensure the fencing is secure and safe around a field or paddock, or that there are no sharp edges or nails sticking out of the wood in his stable.

Help keep your yard tidy so that you avoid any flying paper bags or rubbish, particularly when it is windy. With horses you have to stay alert all the time for things that might alarm them or be potentially dangerous.

If you are planning to stop when out riding, always take a lead rope with you so you can tie your horse or pony somewhere safe and secure.

Never ever tie your horse or pony up with the reins or with a lead rope attached to the bit. If he pulled back he would rip his mouth. Instead, put a halter on as well as a bridle, or attach the rope to the noseband of the bridle.

Always be considerate of other riders.

Acknowledgements

Three years ago when my autobiography was published
I never imagined that I would find myself writing
children's books. Huge thanks go to Louisa Leaman
for helping me to bring Tilly to life, and to
Jennifer Miles for her wonderful illustrations.

Many thanks to Fiona Kennedy for persuading and
encouraging me to search my imagination and for all her
hard work, along with the rest of the team at Orion.
Due to my riding commitments I am not the easiest person
to get hold of as my agent Jonathan Marks
at MTC has found. It's a relief he has been able
to work on all the agreements for me.

Much of my thinking about Tilly has been done
out loud in front of family, friends and godchildren –
thank you all for listening.

More than anything I have to acknowledge my four-legged
friends – my horses. It is thanks to them, and the
great moments I have had with them, that I was able to
create a girl, Tilly, who like me follows her passions.

Pippa Funnell
Forest Green, February 2009

Have read the other *Tilly's Pony Tails* books?

Meet Tilly Redbrow, who doesn't just love horses, she lives, breathes and dreams them too! For every girl who has ever longed for a pony of her own, these delightful, warm and engaging stories are packed with Pippa Funnell's expert advice on everything you ever wanted to know about horses.

LOOK OUT FOR

Pippa Funnell
Follow Your Dreams

Pippa Funnell
as you've never seen her before.

Get to know Pippa – her loves, her hates, her
friends, her family. Meet her beautiful horses,
and take a sneaky peek at life on her gorgeous
farm. Find out how she prepares for important
competitions, trains and cares for her horses, and
still has the time to write *Tilly's Pony Tails*.

And discover how, with hard work, passion
and determination, you too can follow your
dreams, just like Pippa.

978 1 4440 0266 9
£6.99

For more about Tilly and Silver Shoe Farm –
including pony tips, quizzes and everything
you ever wanted to know about horses –
visit www.tillysponytails.co.uk